THE HAPPINESS PROJECT

AASKA SHAH

Made with ❤ on the Notion Press Platform
www.notionpress.com

This book is dedicated to all people who feel alone,
unheard and feel that they have something missing in
their lives, so in case you feel nobody wants to here you,
let me tell you that i am always there no matter what.

Contents

Contents

Contents

Foreword

In a world that constantly tells us what we need to be happy—whether it's the perfect job, the ideal relationship, or the latest material possession—it can be easy to lose sight of the fact that true happiness doesn't come from external circumstances. The truth is, happiness is something we create from within. It's a choice we make each day, in the thoughts we think, the habits we form, and the way we approach life's inevitable ups and downs.

That's where The Happiness Project comes in. This book is not a prescription for a perfect life or a quick fix to all your problems. It's not a checklist of goals to tick off in pursuit of a fleeting happiness. Rather, it is an invitation to transform the way you experience your life, one moment at a time. It is a guide to uncovering the simple, often overlooked, but incredibly powerful practices that can help you cultivate happiness from within.

The Happiness Project is filled with tools and wisdom that anyone can apply, regardless of their circumstances. Whether you're facing challenges, seeking personal growth, or simply looking to live with more peace and joy, this book will help you reconnect with your own capacity for happiness.

One of the key themes of the book is that happiness is not a destination but a journey. It's about developing habits that support your well-being, shifting your perspective to find joy in the everyday moments, and embracing the idea that true happiness comes from living authentically and mindfully.

I have tried to break down complex ideas about happiness into practical steps that anyone can take—no matter where they are on their journey. In these pages, you will find the kind of encouragement, insight, and inspiration that can help you unlock the happiness that already exists within you.

As you read The Happiness Project, remember that this is not a book that promises instant results or guarantees a perfect life. Instead, it is a book that invites you to explore the deeper layers of your own heart and mind, to choose happiness each day, and to embrace the beautiful imperfections that make life truly worth living.

Let this book be a reminder that happiness is not something to be found but something to be created, nurtured, and cherished.

Preface

I began writing as a kid and this is my first book as an author. The main reason for this book was to feel better about myself, as crazy as it sounds but I went through a lot in my life and i just dont want someone else to feel the same way. I want to reach as many people as possible through this book so that they never feel alone and they understand the true essence of happiness.

Happiness—it's a word we all hear often, but how many of us truly understand what it means to live in a state of true joy, fulfillment, and peace? In a world that constantly pulls us in countless directions, where we're often juggling the demands of career, family, and personal growth, it's easy to lose sight of what truly matters. The Happiness Project is my personal journey and exploration of what it takes to cultivate lasting happiness, not as a distant, fleeting emotion but as a deliberate, sustainable state of being.

This project began not as a grand experiment, but rather as a simple question: What if happiness isn't something we find or stumble upon, but something we actively create? Over the course of the next pages, I'll share the lessons I've learned, the experiments I've undertaken, and the tools I've discovered in the quest for a more joyful, meaningful life.

I'm not claiming to have all the answers. What I hope to offer is a roadmap—a guide to help you uncover your own path to happiness. Some of the insights I share may resonate deeply with you, while others may challenge your assumptions. That's part of the process. What I've learned is that happiness is not one-size-fits-all, but a deeply personal, ever-evolving journey.

Whether you've been on a similar quest or are just beginning, my hope is that this book will inspire you to pause, reflect, and take actionable steps toward a life that feels more aligned with who you truly are and what you truly value.

As we embark on this journey together, remember: happiness is not a destination. It is a practice, a mindset, and above all, a choice.

Welcome to The Happiness Project. I'm so glad you're here.

Acknowledgements

This book would not have been possible without the support, encouragement, and wisdom of many people who helped guide me along this journey.

First and foremost, I want to thank my family. To my parents, whose unwavering love and belief in me have been a constant source of inspiration. You've shown me what it means to live with heart, and your support has made every step of this process easier.

To my friends — you've been my sounding boards, my cheerleaders, and my anchors. Thank you for listening without judgment, offering your perspectives, and for reminding me, time and again, that happiness is found not in perfection, but in the simple moments of connection and joy. I am deeply grateful for each of you.

To the countless authors, thinkers, and researchers whose work has inspired me, thank you for your insights and dedication to exploring the depths of human happiness. The knowledge and wisdom shared by these individuals helped lay the foundation for much of this book, and I am deeply grateful for their contributions to the field.

Finally, to you, the reader — thank you for taking this journey with me. It is my deepest hope that the words in this book serve as a source of encouragement and insight, helping you discover your own path to happiness. Your willingness to open your heart and mind to these ideas is the reason I wrote this book in the first place.

Prologue

Happiness is not a distant destination. It's not something we have to wait for or chase outside of ourselves. It's not found in a perfect job, the ideal relationship, or the next accomplishment. True happiness is something we cultivate from within, through the choices we make, the way we think, and how we nurture our inner world.

In our fast-paced world, filled with distractions and endless demands, it's easy to forget this simple truth. We spend so much time striving for more — more success, more possessions, more approval — that we forget happiness is not something to be earned or achieved. It is something to be discovered, nurtured, and experienced every day.

This book is an invitation. An invitation to reconnect with your own potential for joy, peace, and fulfillment. It's a call to shift your focus inward and explore the power you have to shape your emotional and mental landscape. It's an invitation to uncover the tools, practices, and mindsets that can help you create lasting happiness, regardless of life's challenges.

As you turn these pages, you will learn about the science of happiness and how small shifts in mindset, perspective, and behavior can create profound changes in your life. You'll explore the importance of self-compassion, the power of positive habits, and the transformative impact of cultivating a positive mindset. You'll discover how to navigate life's difficulties with resilience, find meaning in your struggles, and build a life filled with gratitude, joy, and connection.

But above all, this book is a reminder that happiness is a journey, not a destination. It's a process of discovering who you are, embracing all of your imperfections, and choosing to live each day with intention. No matter where you are on your path, there's always room to grow, learn, and cultivate more joy.

Are you ready to begin? The journey to happiness starts now — with you, in this moment, on these pages.

CHAPTER I

WHAT IS HAPPINESS

Happiness. It's a word we throw around frequently, but when we stop to truly think about it, how do we define it? Is it a fleeting emotion we feel when things go well? Is it the sense of contentment we experience when life feels balanced? Or is it something deeper—a state of being, a mindset, or a goal we're always striving to reach?

The truth is, happiness means different things to different people, and its definition can be as complex and multifaceted as the individuals who seek it. Throughout history, philosophers, scientists, and writers have attempted to define what it is, what it looks like, and how we can achieve it. And yet, despite the multitude of perspectives, there seems to be a shared consensus: happiness is more than just pleasure or the absence of pain. It's about living a meaningful, fulfilling life that resonates with our deepest values and desires.

CHAPTER II

MYTHS OF HAPPINESS

Myth 1: Happiness is a Destination
One of the biggest misconceptions about happiness is that it's a destination we eventually reach. We often tell ourselves, "I'll be happy when I get that promotion" or "When I find the perfect partner, I'll be happy." In reality, happiness isn't a one-time achievement—it's a journey. It's not about arriving at a certain place in life; it's about how we approach the present moment, regardless of our external circumstances.

Myth 2: Happiness is Out of Our Control
Another myth is that happiness is something that happens to us, based on the people we meet, the job we land, or the experiences we have. While external factors do play a role, research shows that we have much more control over our happiness than we realize. Our mindset, behaviors, and choices can significantly influence our well-being.

Myth 3: Money Equals Happiness
While money can provide security and comfort, research shows that after a certain point, increasing wealth has diminishing returns when it comes to happiness. Once our basic needs are met, the pursuit of material wealth often leads to diminishing returns in terms of long-term happiness. What truly contributes to happiness is not the amount of money we have, but how we use it—whether it's to cultivate experiences, strengthen relationships, or contribute to causes we care about.

So, What Is Happiness?

If happiness is not a simple emotional high or an elusive prize to be won, then what is it? At its core, happiness is a state of well-being that arises from living a life that is aligned with our values, connected to others, and filled with purpose. It's a balance of pleasure and meaning, of striving and enjoying, of engaging with life fully while embracing both its joys and its challenges.

Happiness is personal, and it's a lifelong pursuit. It is not a constant state of bliss, but rather an ongoing process of growth, reflection, and connection. The more we cultivate habits, mindsets, and relationships that support our well-being, the more likely we are to experience the kind of happiness that feels deep and lasting.

CHAPTER III

THE POWER OF MINDSET

If there's one thing that can shape the quality of our lives more than anything else, it's the way we think. Our mindset—how we approach life, interpret our experiences, and view our potential—has a profound influence on our happiness. In fact, studies show that our mindset can determine not only how we feel in the moment but how we navigate challenges, set goals, and build meaningful relationships.

While we often think of our external circumstances as the primary drivers of our happiness, the truth is, it's how we respond to those circumstances that matters most. A positive mindset doesn't mean ignoring reality or putting on a false smile. It means cultivating a mindset that empowers us to see opportunities for growth, learning, and joy, no matter what life throws our way.

If we are not strong enough mentally, there is no space for us in this world. There are going to be times when someone or something that we thought we would never lose, is lost, and we are going to feel terrible about it. Its okay, we're human and its normal to cry the full day, miss them frequently but i want you to ask yourself this one question. Was that person worth your energy? If the answer is yes, go ahead, continue chasing them but if the answer is no, you got to stop. You have much better things in your life to focus on and you have better people in your life that genuinely care about you so spend your energy on those people and not the ones who treated you like trash.

CHAPTER IV

CONTROL

THE UNIVERSE IS NOT IN YOUR CONTROL.

Things are going to come your way only when they have to and only when you're ready for them.

Stop caring about things that are never going to be in your control

One of the most powerful realizations on the path to happiness is the understanding that, despite our best efforts, there are many things in life that we cannot control. Whether it's the actions of others, the weather, or the unexpected twists and turns of life, much of what happens to us is outside our direct influence.

The Things You Can't Control

Here are a few areas of life where it's important to recognize that control is limited or nonexistent:

1. The Past

No matter how much we wish we could rewrite our history, the past is beyond our control. We cannot change the decisions we made, the mistakes we made, or the things that happened to us. Yet, many people spend an inordinate amount of energy ruminating on what could have been. This focus on the past can prevent us from moving forward and embracing the present moment. True happiness lies not in altering the past, but in accepting it, learning from it, and using it to shape a better future.

2. Other People's Actions and Opinions

No matter how hard we try, we cannot control the behavior, beliefs, or opinions of others. People will act based on their own values, experiences, and emotions. We can influence, persuade, and communicate, but ultimately, their choices are not within our power.

This is especially relevant in relationships. We may wish our partner, friend, or family member would change, but forcing change on others usually leads to frustration. Instead, the key to happiness in relationships is acceptance: embracing people as they are while setting healthy boundaries around how we allow their actions to impact us.

3. The Future

We often spend a great deal of time worrying about what will happen tomorrow, next year, or in the distant future. Yet, the future is full of uncertainty, and no amount of planning or worrying can change that. This uncertainty can cause stress, anxiety, and a sense of helplessness. The more we try to control the future, the more we miss out on the present moment.

Happiness comes from living in the here and now—taking actions today that are aligned with our values, without obsessing over the outcomes. It's about releasing the need for certainty and embracing the unknown with openness and flexibility.

4. Natural Events and the World Around Us

While we can take steps to protect the environment and prepare for natural disasters, much of the world's natural processes are beyond our control. The weather, seasons, and natural events like earthquakes or floods remind us that, despite all our technological advances, there are forces far bigger than ourselves.

Learning to navigate life with the acceptance that some things—like a rainy day, a health crisis, or a global event—are out of our hands helps us to better handle stress and maintain our sense of peace when unexpected challenges arise.

5. Health and Aging

Our bodies are remarkable, but they are not invincible. Despite our best efforts, we cannot control how our bodies age, when we fall ill, or the genetic predispositions we inherit. The struggle to maintain perfect health can be exhausting and disheartening, especially when we face a diagnosis or physical limitations.

Instead of focusing on controlling our health in ways that are unrealistic, we can focus on taking care of our bodies in ways that support vitality and well-being. This means eating nourishing foods, exercising regularly, and managing stress, but also accepting that some aspects of our health will always be beyond our control.

6. *Luck and Circumstance*

Life's randomness—whether it's winning the lottery, receiving an unexpected opportunity, or experiencing a sudden setback—reminds us that so much of what happens to us is based on chance. While we can create conditions that increase our likelihood of success, luck still plays a significant role in the trajectory of our lives.

Instead of being resentful about the role of luck, happiness comes from cultivating a mindset that appreciates what we have and maximizes what is within our control. By embracing the unpredictability of life, we free ourselves from the need for certainty and open ourselves to new opportunities.

Letting Go: The Path to Freedom

Accepting that there are things beyond our control is not a passive act. It's an empowering choice. The freedom comes when we stop resisting and start focusing on what we can change—our responses, our mindset, and our actions.

For example, when we let go of our need to control other people's actions or opinions, we can focus on cultivating healthier, more authentic relationships. When we let go of the pressure to be perfect or in control of every detail of our lives, we make room for more creativity, spontaneity, and peace of mind.

The Importance of Acceptance

Acceptance doesn't mean resignation or giving up—it means making peace with the things that are outside our control and choosing to focus on how we react. One of the best ways to practice acceptance is to ask yourself:

What am I spending energy on that I cannot control?

How can I reframe my perspective to focus on what I can change?

What would it feel like to let go of the need to control this situation?

By consciously releasing our grip on the uncontrollable, we open ourselves to a sense of freedom and calm. We allow ourselves to live with less stress and more joy, knowing that we are actively choosing where to invest our energy.

Its okay if you were in a relationship with the wrong person. I know that person treated you wrongly and you did not deserve it at all. You deserve so much better and you know you are capable of it. Just because one person treated you wrongly doesn't mean everyone is the same. You just have to believe in the universe and your destiny and everything else comes along. If not today, tomorrow for sure!

CHAPTER V

FAILURE

Failure. It's a word that often carries a heavy weight, one that many of us fear or try to avoid at all costs. From the time we are children, we're conditioned to avoid failure—to succeed, to achieve, and to be perfect. But what if I told you that failure is not only inevitable, but that it's also one of the most powerful forces for growth, happiness, and transformation?

The truth is, failure is not the opposite of success—it's a part of success. Every person who has ever achieved anything meaningful has encountered failure. From world-class athletes to entrepreneurs, scientists to artists, failure has been an integral part of their journey. It's not the failure itself that determines our future, but how we respond to it.

THE FEAR OF FAILURE

Most of us are terrified of failing. We fear what others will think of us, what it will mean about our abilities, or how it will affect our future opportunities. This fear can paralyze us and prevent us from taking risks, trying new things, or stepping out of our comfort zones. We might choose the safer path, avoid challenges, or stay in situations that feel familiar—because the alternative might involve the dreaded prospect of failing.

But this fear of failure often keeps us from experiencing the full potential of our lives. It keeps us small, playing it safe and avoiding the very experiences that can lead to growth. The irony is that, by avoiding failure, we often avoid the very successes that are waiting for us just on the other side

A failure doesnt define who you are. It simply means that you are destined for something much better and bigger. You can have multiple failures and multiple mental breakdowns. You can cry and crib about it for months but is it going to make it any better? No right? Then make the best of the situation that you have at present and focus of making your future better

REFRAMING OF FAILURE

To shift our perspective on failure, we need to reframe how we think about it. Instead of viewing failure as a negative event or something to be ashamed of, let's think of it as feedback—a tool for learning and growth. Every failure carries with it valuable lessons that can guide us toward success. It shows us what doesn't work, so we can try something different next time.

Consider Thomas Edison's famous quote about his many failed attempts to create the light bulb:
"I have not failed. I've just found 10,000 ways that won't work."

In this reframing, failure becomes an integral part of the process of discovering what will work. It is not an end, but a step toward improvement, innovation, and mastery. The more we fail, the more we learn—and the closer we get to achieving our goals.

Why Failure Is Essential for Growth

Failure Builds Resilience
Failure teaches us how to bounce back, how to pick ourselves up after a setback, and how to keep going when things get tough. Resilience is one of the key traits that separate those who succeed in life from those who give up after encountering obstacles. Every failure is an opportunity to build emotional strength and perseverance.

Resilience doesn't mean never feeling down or discouraged—it means developing the capacity to recover and keep moving forward. When we embrace failure as part of the journey, we become more adaptable and confident in our ability to handle whatever life throws at us.

Failure Encourages Innovation and Creativity
When something doesn't work out, it forces us to think differently, approach problems from new angles, and find creative solutions. Many of the world's greatest innovations—be it in science, art, or technology—have come from the willingness to fail and iterate. The key is to keep experimenting, even when things don't go as planned.

Take the example of J.K. Rowling, who faced numerous rejections before Harry Potter became a global phenomenon. Had she given up after the first, second, or tenth rejection, the world would have missed out on one of the most beloved book series of all time.

Failure Fosters Humility

Failure is humbling. It reminds us that we are not invincible, and that we don't have all the answers. This humility can actually be a source of happiness, because it frees us from the constant pressure to be perfect or to have everything under control. We learn that it's okay to not have all the answers, and that asking for help, being vulnerable, and learning from others is part of what makes us human.

Embracing failure with humility helps us build stronger connections with others and fosters a sense of shared experience. No one is exempt from failure, and recognizing that can help us feel more connected and less isolated in our struggles.

Failure Leads to Self-Discovery

Each time we fail, we are presented with a chance to learn more about ourselves—our strengths, our weaknesses, our passions, and our values. Failure forces us to confront our limitations and consider what's truly important to us. In this process of self-reflection, we discover who we are and what we want out of life.

Sometimes, failure can even help us realize that our original goal wasn't what we truly wanted or needed. It can redirect us toward a path that is more aligned with our authentic selves. The detours created by failure often

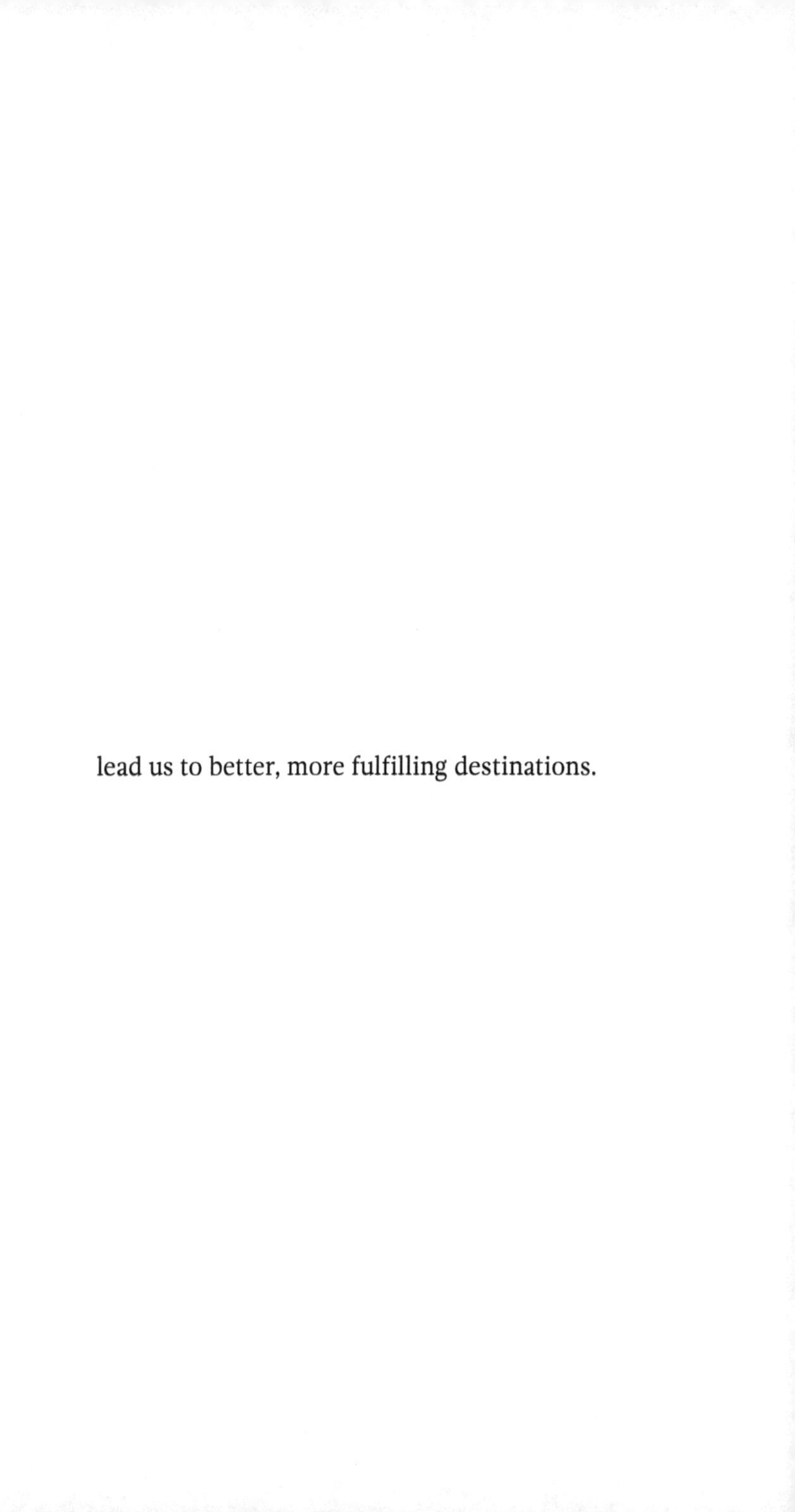

lead us to better, more fulfilling destinations.

Shifting from Perfectionism to Progress

One of the biggest obstacles to embracing failure is our culture's obsession with perfectionism. We are taught to strive for flawless outcomes, to meet expectations, and to succeed without faltering. Perfectionism, however, is often rooted in a deep fear of failure. It creates an unrealistic standard that makes us paralyzed by the prospect of not being "good enough."

Instead of aiming for perfection, we can shift our focus to progress. Progress is about moving forward, learning from each experience, and growing from every step—no matter how imperfect. Progress embraces the idea that each small step, each failure, and each lesson learned brings us closer to where we want to be.

When we focus on progress instead of perfection, we free ourselves from the pressure to be perfect and allow ourselves the freedom to fail, learn, and try again. This mindset makes the journey itself enjoyable, rather than stressing about the destination.

How to Embrace Failure in a Healthy Way

Change Your Narrative

Start by changing the story you tell yourself about failure. Instead of saying, "I failed," try saying, "I learned something valuable today." Reframe each failure as an opportunity for growth. The more you change the narrative, the more natural it will feel to embrace failure as part of the process.

Learn to Detach Your Self-Worth from Success

Failure can sting, especially if we tie our self-worth to our achievements. But remember: failing does not mean you are a failure. Separate your identity from your outcomes. You are not defined by your success or your failures—you are defined by your willingness to keep going, to learn, and to evolve.

Celebrate Failure

This might sound counterintuitive, but celebrating failure can help you view it in a more positive light. Reflect on the lessons you've learned, the resilience you've built, and the growth you've experienced. You can also celebrate small wins along the way, acknowledging the effort and progress you've made, even if the ultimate goal is still out of reach.

Practice Self-Compassion

Be kind to yourself when things don't go as planned.

Instead of beating yourself up, practice self-compassion. Treat yourself with the same understanding and encouragement you would offer to a friend who is struggling. Failure is hard, but it's much easier to move forward when we treat ourselves with care and empathy.

Take Action Anyway
Ultimately, the best way to overcome the fear of failure is to take action despite it. Step outside your comfort zone. Take risks. The more you experience failure, the more you'll realize it's not the end of the world—it's simply part of the journey.

Failure is not the end—it's a stepping stone on the path to growth and happiness. Every failure teaches us something valuable, whether it's about ourselves, our goals, or the world around us. By embracing failure, we free ourselves from the fear of making mistakes and open ourselves to a richer, more fulfilling life.

The key is not to avoid failure, but to use it. Each failure is a lesson. Each setback is an opportunity to try again, to innovate, and to become stronger. So, the next time you face failure, remember this: it's not the end of your story—it's the beginning of your next chapter.

CHAPTER VI

BREAKUPS

One of life's most universally painful experiences is a breakup. Whether it's the end of a romantic relationship, the loss of a friendship, or even the dissolution of a business partnership, the emotional weight of letting go can feel overwhelming. Breakups often bring a flood of conflicting emotions—heartache, confusion, anger, loneliness, and sometimes even relief. In the aftermath, we may find ourselves questioning everything: our choices, our self-worth, and our future.

But while breakups are painful, they also have the potential to be powerful catalysts for growth. They can teach us important lessons about ourselves, help us reevaluate what we truly want in relationships, and ultimately pave the way for healing, self-love, and the discovery of new opportunities.

The Emotional Rollercoaster of Breakups

When a relationship ends, it's common to experience a whirlwind of emotions. While everyone processes breakups differently, there are a few key emotional stages that many people go through. These stages are similar to the grief process, as we mourn the loss of what could have been, and the dream of a future with that person.

Shock and Denial

At first, the reality of the breakup may feel surreal. You may find yourself in a state of disbelief, struggling to accept that the relationship is truly over. Denial can be a defense mechanism, as your mind tries to protect you from the emotional pain that's coming. During this stage, you might find yourself replaying conversations or situations over and over, trying to make sense of it all.

Sadness and Grief

As the shock begins to wear off, the sadness sets in. Grief is a natural response to loss, and even if the relationship wasn't perfect, you're mourning the connection, the shared experiences, and the plans you had for the future. This period can be especially challenging if the breakup was unexpected or if you still have strong feelings for the other person.

Anger and Resentment

As the reality of the breakup sets in, feelings of anger or

resentment can surface. You might feel betrayed, frustrated, or even blame yourself for the end of the relationship. Sometimes, these feelings can be directed toward the other person, especially if there were unresolved issues or if the breakup felt unfair.

Fear and Anxiety

After a breakup, there's often a fear of being alone or an anxiety about what the future holds. You might wonder if you'll ever find love again, or if you made a mistake by letting go. These feelings can create a sense of uncertainty, and it may be difficult to imagine life without that person by your side.

Acceptance and Healing

Eventually, as time passes, acceptance begins to emerge. This doesn't mean that the pain instantly disappears, but it's a sign that you're beginning to come to terms with the end of the relationship. You may start to see the breakup as an opportunity for growth, personal exploration, and the chance to rebuild your life in a way that's aligned with your needs and desires.

ALLOW YOURSELF TO GRIEVE

It's easy to want to rush through the pain of a breakup and get back to "normal" as quickly as possible. But healing from a breakup takes time, and it's important to allow yourself to grieve. Just like any other loss, the end of a relationship involves mourning the loss of a connection, a future, and often an identity you built around that person. You dont have to be hard on yourself! Its okay, breathe!

You dont need to move on today itself, in fact you cannot. That person was your entire world a while ago and they are gone out of your life as if nothing ever happened. It feels pathetic, trust me i know what you're feeling. 'Why did we ever be together if we weren't meant to be' , ' Am i not good enough'. Thinking all of this is natural and is a part of the healing process. Its not important for you to have all your questions answered but let me tell you one thing, *YOU ARE GOOD ENOUGH AND THINGS DID NOT WORK OUT BECAUSE YOU DESERVE SOMEONE WHO HAS THE SAME ENERGY AND POSITIVITY AS YOU AND YOUR EX JUST CAME IN YOUR LIFE TO TEACH YOU NOT TO CHOOSE THE WRONG ONES!*

DISCOVER 'YOU'

One of the most empowering aspects of a breakup is the opportunity it offers for self-discovery and personal growth. When a relationship ends, you're left with space to rediscover who you are outside of that connection. This can be a time to reflect on your values, your goals, and your desires.

Reevaluating What You Want

A breakup provides the perfect opportunity to take a step back and reassess what you truly want in a relationship. What were the aspects of the relationship that brought you joy, and what were the parts that left you feeling unfulfilled? What qualities are most important to you in a partner? Understanding what worked and what didn't can help you make better choices in future relationships.

Rediscovering Yourself

Often, in long-term relationships, we become so intertwined with our partner's identity that we lose touch with our own. After a breakup, you have the chance to reconnect with yourself, explore your own passions, and rediscover what makes you happy. This process of self-discovery can be deeply liberating and can help you cultivate a stronger sense of independence and self-worth.

Setting Boundaries and Standards

WHY DID YOU LOWER YOUR STANDARDS FOR THAT ONE PERSON WHEN YOU WERE SO MUCH BETTER? Its okay now you've learnt your lesson so never make that mistake again.

HEAL

Healing from a breakup is a process, but there are practical steps you can take to support your emotional recovery:

Lean on Your Support System
Surround yourself with people who care about you—friends, family, or trusted confidants. Talking about your feelings, venting, or simply having someone to listen can make a huge difference in the healing process. Don't be afraid to ask for support when you need it, and allow others to remind you of your worth during this difficult time.

Practice Self-Care
Self-care is essential for emotional healing. Take time to nurture yourself physically, emotionally, and mentally. This might include getting enough rest, eating nourishing foods, exercising, meditating, or engaging in activities that make you feel good. Doing things that make you feel whole again can help restore your sense of balance and well-being.

Create Space for New Experiences
One of the most powerful ways to heal from a breakup is to create new experiences for yourself. Travel, start a new hobby, meet new people, or simply try something you've never done before. By shifting your focus to new, positive experiences, you create fresh memories that help diminish the pain of the past.

Reflect, Don't Ruminate
While reflection is a healthy way to understand what happened in the relationship, ruminating or obsessing over the past can keep you stuck. It's important to allow yourself space to reflect on the lessons, but also to let go of the need for answers. Sometimes, closure comes not from knowing why things happened, but from deciding to move forward regardless.

Allow Yourself to Love Again (When You're Ready)
After a breakup, you may wonder if you'll ever be able to love again. The answer is yes—but only when you're ready. Give yourself permission to heal fully before jumping into a new relationship. True healing comes when you've rediscovered your sense of self, healed from the past, and are open to the possibility of new love without comparison to the past.

LET GO

Breakups are undoubtedly painful, but they also offer a unique opportunity to let go of what no longer serves us. Letting go can be an act of self-compassion, a sign that you're prioritizing your own growth, happiness, and emotional well-being.

Letting go of a relationship doesn't mean erasing the love you once shared, but rather accepting that sometimes things end for a reason. By allowing yourself to grieve, learn, and grow, you create space for new beginnings—whether that's a new relationship, a deeper connection with yourself, or a more fulfilling life overall.

In the end, breakups teach us that we are resilient. We can heal, we can learn, and we can thrive after loss. Every ending brings with it the possibility of a new beginning. And in the process, we discover that true happiness doesn't depend on any one relationship—it depends on the relationship we have with ourselves.

CHAPTER VII

FRIENDSHIPS

Friendship is one of life's greatest gifts. It provides companionship, support, laughter, and a sense of belonging. Friends are the people we turn to in times of joy and sorrow, the ones who see us at our best and our worst, and yet choose to stay by our side. In many ways, friendships form the foundation of our emotional well-being and play a crucial role in our happiness.

But just like any relationship, friendships can be complicated. They require effort, communication, and mutual respect to thrive. As we go through different stages of life, we may find that our friendships evolve, and sometimes even fade.

THE FRIENDSHIP TEST

While friendships can be a source of immense joy, they are not always easy. Just like any other relationship, friendships come with challenges. Life changes, misunderstandings occur, and sometimes people grow apart. Navigating these challenges can feel painful, but it's also an opportunity to learn, grow, and reevaluate what you want from your friendships.

Growing Apart

Over time, it's natural for friendships to evolve. As we grow, change jobs, move to different places, or go through different life experiences, our needs and priorities shift. Sometimes, friendships simply run their course. This doesn't necessarily mean that the friendship was less important—it just may not align with your current life. If you find yourself drifting apart from a friend, it's important to acknowledge it and decide whether to invest time in rekindling the connection or gracefully let go.

Conflict and Misunderstandings

Conflict is inevitable in any relationship, including friendships. If a disagreement arises, approach it with a mindset of resolution rather than blame. Communication is key—try to listen to your friend's perspective, express your own feelings calmly, and work together to find a solution. Sometimes, taking a step back to cool off can help, but be sure to address issues before they fester into resentment.

Toxic Friendships
Not all friendships are healthy. In some cases, you may find that a friend is draining, unsupportive, or even toxic. Toxic friendships can leave you feeling emotionally exhausted, unappreciated, or worse—undermined. It's important to recognize when a friendship is no longer serving you and to set boundaries or, if necessary, walk away. Cutting ties with a toxic friend is difficult, but it's essential for your own emotional health and happiness. Remember, true friends build each other up, not tear each other down.

Feeling Lonely or Left Out
Sometimes, even with close friends, we can experience feelings of loneliness or isolation. These feelings are valid and should not be ignored. If you're feeling disconnected, try to reach out to your friends and share how you're feeling. If necessary, seek out new opportunities to meet people and form connections. It's okay to acknowledge that you need more support or new social circles. Friendships take effort, and it's important to find the right balance of give and take.

TOXIC FRIENDSHIPS

Not all friendships are healthy. While most of us know the joy and support that comes from a true, loving friend, there are also friendships that can leave us feeling drained, unappreciated, or even emotionally harmed. These friendships can be toxic—relationships that do not nourish us, but rather, cause harm, undermine our confidence, and negatively affect our well-being.

Toxic friendships can be especially difficult to recognize, especially when the person involved is someone you've known for a long time, or when there is an emotional bond that makes it hard to let go. But understanding what constitutes a toxic friendship, how it impacts our happiness, and how to set healthy boundaries or move on from such relationships is crucial for our emotional and mental health.

IMPACT OF TOXIC FRIENDSHIPS

Decreased Self-Esteem

Being around someone who constantly undermines you, criticizes you, or makes you feel unworthy can chip away at your self-esteem. You may start questioning your own value or feel like you're not good enough, especially if the toxic friend's behavior leaves you feeling inadequate or judged.

Increased Stress and Anxiety

The constant drama and emotional manipulation that often come with toxic friendships can lead to heightened levels of stress and anxiety. You may feel tense or on edge whenever you're around the toxic friend, or you might experience a sense of dread before meeting up with them. Over time, this chronic stress can affect your physical health and overall sense of well-being.

Isolation

Sometimes, toxic friends can isolate you from other people. They may subtly encourage you to cut ties with other friends or create an unhealthy dependence on them. In extreme cases, they may try to make you feel guilty for spending time with other people, leading you to feel isolated or trapped in the relationship.

Emotional Drainage

A friendship that constantly demands emotional labor

without reciprocating it can leave you feeling drained. The emotional work required to support a toxic friend, or to navigate their manipulative or demanding behavior, can be exhausting. Over time, you may find yourself feeling empty, as though you are giving all of your energy to someone who is not giving anything back.

Lowered Happiness and Joy
When you're in a toxic friendship, it can feel like a cloud hanging over your life. You may lose the ability to experience joy or feel as though you're always "on edge." The constant negativity, drama, and emotional strain caused by the toxic friendship can make it harder to appreciate the good things in life, ultimately diminishing your overall sense of happiness.

Do you ever feel like oh i wish that person was yet in my life and i could still count on them? Well its really normal to miss them, but when you needed them the most, where were they? Did they stand by you? Did they support you? Did they hear you out? Did they protect you? Well if the answer is yes, get them back but if the answer is no, Its time to let go. They were removed from your life because you wouldn't let anything happen to them and would stand by them even in a crowd of millions of people but they wouldn't do even ten percent of what you would.

Letting Go for Your Happiness

It's hard to let go of a friendship, especially when there's a history involved, or if the friendship has moments of positivity. But remember that your happiness, peace of mind, and emotional health are more important than maintaining a toxic relationship out of guilt, obligation, or fear of confrontation. True friends lift you up, support you, and make you feel good about yourself—anything less is not worth holding onto.

Sometimes, the kindest thing you can do for both yourself and your toxic friend is to let go. Allow yourself the space to heal, grow, and make room for friendships that nourish and empower you. Your true friends will be there when you need them, and you will find that letting go of toxic relationships opens up space for deeper, more authentic connections.

CHAPTER VIII

Self-Love – The Foundation of True Happiness

At the heart of lasting happiness lies an often overlooked yet deeply powerful practice: self-love. Many of us seek validation and love from others, hoping that external approval will bring us the fulfillment we crave. Yet, true happiness can never be found solely in the validation of others; it must begin within. When we cultivate self-love, we create a strong foundation for emotional well-being, confidence, and resilience in the face of life's challenges.

Self-love is not just about indulging in self-care or treating ourselves to occasional pleasures. It's a mindset, a set of practices, and a deep respect for who we are, in all our imperfections. It means accepting ourselves as we are, while also nurturing our growth and potential. In this chapter, we'll explore the importance of self-love, the common obstacles to developing it, and practical ways to cultivate a deeper sense of love and compassion for ourselves.

WHAT IS SELF LOVE?

Self-love is often misunderstood as selfishness or arrogance. However, it's quite the opposite. True self-love means recognizing your intrinsic value and worth, independent of your achievements, appearance, or the opinions of others. It's about honoring your needs, setting boundaries, forgiving yourself for past mistakes, and celebrating your own uniqueness.

Self-love is the foundation upon which all other forms of love and connection can flourish. When we love ourselves, we set a powerful example for others about how to treat us. We teach others to value and respect us, and in turn, we attract healthier, more positive relationships into our lives.

IMPORTANCE OF SELF LOVE

Self-love is not just a feel-good concept; it is essential to our overall happiness and well-being. Here are a few reasons why self-love is key to living a fulfilled life:

Increases Self-Worth and Confidence

When you love yourself, you develop a strong sense of self-worth. You stop relying on external validation to feel good about yourself, and instead, you affirm your value from within. This inner confidence allows you to take on new challenges, pursue your goals, and trust in your own abilities.

Promotes Emotional Resilience

Self-love gives you the emotional resilience to handle life's inevitable setbacks and disappointments. When you face challenges with a healthy sense of self-worth, you're less likely to be shaken by failure or criticism. You learn to bounce back more quickly, knowing that your value isn't defined by a single outcome or experience.

Fosters Healthy Relationships

When you love yourself, you are more likely to attract and maintain healthy relationships. Self-love empowers you to set boundaries, communicate openly, and avoid toxic dynamics. It also allows you to give and receive love in a balanced, fulfilling way, rather than depending on others for validation.

Reduces Negative Self-Talk

One of the most damaging things we can do is criticize or berate ourselves. Negative self-talk is often rooted in insecurity or fear of judgment. Cultivating self-love helps you replace these harsh thoughts with kindness and compassion. You begin to treat yourself with the same empathy and understanding that you would offer a close friend.

Encourages Personal Growth

Loving yourself means accepting yourself as you are, but it also means recognizing the potential for growth and improvement. You approach your personal development with patience and curiosity, knowing that you are worthy of the effort. When we approach our goals from a place of self-love, rather than self-criticism, we are more likely to succeed and experience lasting change.

BARRIERS TO SELF LOVE

Here are some common barriers to self-love:

Perfectionism

Perfectionism is a major obstacle to self-love. The belief that you must be perfect in every area of your life can lead to constant self-criticism and feelings of inadequacy. Perfectionism creates unrealistic standards, and when you inevitably fall short of them, it chips away at your self-worth.

Comparison to Others

In the age of social media, it's easy to fall into the trap of comparing yourself to others. We often look at the highlight reels of other people's lives and believe that we are somehow lacking. Constant comparison can lead to feelings of jealousy, inadequacy, and low self-esteem. The truth is, everyone has their own unique journey, and no one's life is as perfect as it may appear online.

Fear of Judgment

Many people struggle with self-love because they fear judgment or rejection from others. We may worry that loving ourselves too much will make us seem arrogant or self-centered. The reality is that loving yourself is the healthiest thing you can do for yourself, and it actually helps you show up more authentically in your relationships and work.

<u>**Unhealed Past Trauma**</u>

Past wounds and unresolved trauma can also create barriers to self-love. If we've been hurt or neglected in the past, we may carry those wounds with us and struggle to feel deserving of love or care. Healing from past pain takes time, but it is possible with the right tools and support. Self-love involves not just accepting who you are today, but also acknowledging and healing from your past.

<u>**Low Self-Worth**</u>

Some individuals struggle with low self-worth because of childhood experiences, societal conditioning, or repeated failures. When you don't feel worthy of love, it's difficult to offer it to yourself. Overcoming this barrier requires compassion, self-acceptance, and, often, professional support to shift deeply ingrained beliefs.

CULTIVATING SELF LOVE

Cultivating self-love is a gradual process, and it requires consistent practice and self-compassion. Here are some practical steps you can take to develop a deeper sense of love and respect for yourself:

Practice Self-Compassion

When you make a mistake or experience failure, respond to yourself with compassion instead of self-criticism. Treat yourself the way you would treat a friend who is going through a tough time—offer kindness, encouragement, and understanding. Remind yourself that you are only human, and imperfections are a part of life.

Set Boundaries

Setting boundaries is an act of self-respect. When you set limits on what you will and won't tolerate from others, you are protecting your emotional energy and demonstrating self-love. Boundaries help you prioritize your well-being and prevent burnout from overcommitting or allowing others to take advantage of your time and resources.

Engage in Activities that Nourish You

Take time to engage in activities that make you feel good—whether it's a hobby, physical activity, creative outlet, or simply relaxing. Do things that nurture your body, mind, and soul. When you engage in self-care activities, you reinforce the idea that you are worthy of love and attention.

Affirm Your Worth

One powerful practice to boost self-love is the use of affirmations. Positive affirmations help rewire negative thought patterns and reinforce a healthy self-image. Daily affirmations such as "I am worthy of love," "I am enough," or "I deserve happiness" can help shift your mindset over time.

Stop People-Pleasing

People-pleasing is a form of self-sacrifice that can undermine your sense of self-worth. When you constantly put others' needs before your own, you neglect your own well-being. Learn to say no when necessary, and recognize that it's okay to prioritize yourself. Saying no is not selfish—it's an essential part of maintaining your mental and emotional health.

Forgive Yourself

One of the most transformative aspects of self-love is self-forgiveness. Let go of past mistakes, regrets, or failures. Understand that you did the best you could with the knowledge and resources you had at the time. Forgiving yourself frees you from the burden of guilt and allows you to move forward with a sense of peace.

Surround Yourself with Positive Influences

Surround yourself with people who uplift and support you, and distance yourself from those who bring negativity or doubt. Positive relationships encourage self-love by reaffirming your worth and encouraging you to be your best self.

CHAPTER IX

YOU ARE YOUR OWN BEST FRIEND

In the quest for happiness, there is one truth that stands above all else: you are your own best friend. While we seek companionship, validation, and support from others, it's easy to forget that the most important relationship we will ever have is the one with ourselves.

In a world that constantly tells us to compare ourselves to others, meet external expectations, and live up to societal standards, the idea of being our own best friend may sound like a radical concept. But it is precisely through the practice of self-love—through treating ourselves with the same kindness, respect, and care that we would offer to a cherished friend—that we unlock the door to true, lasting happiness.

Being your own best friend means having your own back, no matter what. It's about offering yourself unwavering support, kindness, and acceptance. Just like a best friend would encourage you to go after your dreams, forgive yourself when you mess up, and remind you of your worth when you feel low, you can be that person for yourself.

To be your own best friend, you must:

Embrace self-compassion – Rather than criticizing yourself for mistakes or shortcomings, you offer yourself kindness and understanding. A best friend wouldn't berate you for a slip-up, and neither should you.

Celebrate your victories – Just like a best friend would cheer you on in your successes, it's essential that you learn to celebrate your own achievements, big or small.

Set boundaries for your own well-being – A good friend always respects your boundaries, and so should you. Learn to say no when needed and prioritize your own needs.

Forgive yourself – A best friend would never hold grudges against you; they would forgive you, no matter what. Similarly, when you make mistakes, offer yourself the same grace.

Show up for yourself – Whether things are going well or you're struggling, you show up for yourself with love, understanding, and support, just as you would for a friend

who needs you.

WHY DO YOU HAVE TO BE YOUR OWN BEST FRIEND?

You may wonder, why is it so important to become your own best friend? Aren't relationships with others enough? The answer is: no, they're not.

The relationships we have with others, whether friends, family, or partners, are deeply meaningful. But no one can make us feel whole or worthy if we don't first believe those things about ourselves. The way we treat ourselves sets the tone for how others treat us and how we allow ourselves to be treated. If we don't practice self-love and self-compassion, it becomes harder to attract healthy, supportive relationships.

You Are the Only Constant in Your Life

People come and go, but you will always be with yourself. Your relationship with yourself is the longest and most enduring relationship you will ever have. When you learn to nurture that relationship, you create stability and inner peace. Even in the toughest moments, you'll have yourself to lean on.

Self-Compassion Enhances Resilience

Life throws curveballs at us all the time, whether in the form of failure, disappointment, or unexpected challenges. When we treat ourselves as our own best friend, we can weather these storms with resilience. We give ourselves permission to make mistakes and grow from them, rather than spiral into shame or self-blame.

Your Self-Worth Doesn't Depend on Others

When you are your own best friend, your sense of worth is not dependent on external validation or approval. You validate yourself. You recognize your value, not because of your achievements or how others see you, but simply because you exist. This deep sense of self-worth frees you from the burden of trying to please others or earn their love and acceptance.

You Model Healthy Relationships for Others

The way you treat yourself is a reflection of how you teach others to treat you. If you value yourself and set healthy boundaries, you inspire others to do the same. You attract relationships that are nurturing and positive because you've learned to show up for yourself with love and respect.

<u>Self-Love Fosters Inner Peace</u>

When you treat yourself as your own best friend, you cultivate a sense of inner peace and contentment. You stop worrying about what others think, stop striving for perfection, and stop feeling the need to meet unrealistic expectations. You become at ease with who you are, flaws and all, and that acceptance leads to peace.

HOW TO BECOME YOUR BEST FRIEND?

Speak to Yourself Kindly

Imagine you're having a conversation with your best friend. Would you call them names or criticize them harshly? Likely not. Now, consider how you talk to yourself on a daily basis. Are your thoughts kind and supportive, or are you overly critical?

Start by replacing negative self-talk with kind and encouraging words. When you catch yourself being hard on yourself, stop and reframe your thoughts. For example, instead of saying, "I'm so stupid for making that mistake," say, "I made a mistake, but I'm learning and growing."

Forgive Yourself for Past Mistakes

Everyone makes mistakes, and one of the greatest acts of self-love is forgiveness. If you've been carrying guilt or regret for past decisions, let it go. Forgiveness frees you from the weight of the past and allows you to move forward. Treat yourself with the same compassion you would offer a friend who has made a mistake.

Prioritize Your Own Needs

Being your own best friend means making time for your own needs, even when life gets busy. Whether it's taking a walk, reading a book, or simply sitting in silence, give yourself the time and space to recharge. Don't feel guilty for saying "no" to others when it means saying "yes" to yourself.

Celebrate Your Wins

Just as a best friend would cheer for your accomplishments, make sure to celebrate your own successes. It doesn't matter how big or small the achievement is—acknowledge it. Take a moment to appreciate your hard work and the progress you've made. This reinforces your sense of self-worth and reminds you of how capable you are.

Set Boundaries and Protect Your Peace

As your own best friend, you must protect your peace. This means setting boundaries with people and situations that drain your energy or bring negativity into your life. A best friend would tell you to walk away from toxic situations—do the same for yourself. Learn to say no when something doesn't serve your well-being.

Take Care of Your Body and Mind

Your best friend wouldn't let you neglect your health. They'd encourage you to eat well, get enough sleep, and engage in activities that nourish your body and mind. Make self-care a priority, not just as a form of pampering, but as an act of deep respect for yourself.

Be Patient with Yourself

Just as you would support a friend through their ups and downs, be patient with yourself as you navigate life's challenges. You are allowed to grow, to make mistakes, and to take things one step at a time. Self-love isn't about being perfect; it's about being kind to yourself, especially

when you're struggling.

LOVE YOURSELF LIKE YOUR BEST FRIEND

The key to happiness isn't found in the approval of others, nor in the pursuit of external goals or possessions. It's found in the relationship you have with yourself. When you become your own best friend, you no longer depend on others to define your worth. You become your own source of love, encouragement, and support.

Remember, you are worthy of the same kindness, compassion, and respect that you offer to your closest friends. By treating yourself as your own best friend, you create a deep sense of inner peace and happiness that no one can take away.

So today, choose to be your own best friend. Choose to love yourself, support yourself, and show up for yourself. Your happiness begins within.

CHAPTER X

GRATITUDE

One of the simplest yet most profound ways to increase happiness is by embracing gratitude. It's easy to overlook this powerful tool in the pursuit of happiness, especially when we're caught up in the whirlwind of daily life. But when we take a moment to truly reflect on what we have, rather than focusing on what we lack, we unlock an entirely new level of joy and contentment.

Gratitude is not just a feel-good concept; it is a scientifically backed practice that can rewire your brain, improve your relationships, and enhance your overall well-being. When we cultivate a mindset of gratitude, we shift our focus from scarcity to abundance, from what's wrong in our lives to what's going right. In doing so, we become more resilient, more positive, and ultimately, more happy.

WHAT IS GRATITUDE?

Gratitude is the practice of recognizing and appreciating the good things in our lives—whether big or small. It's about acknowledging the moments, people, and experiences that bring us joy and fulfillment, and expressing our thanks for them. In its most basic form, gratitude is an act of noticing the positive in our lives, even when life feels overwhelming or challenging.

Gratitude is not just about being thankful for obvious blessings like health, family, or success. It's about finding joy in the seemingly mundane—like a warm cup of coffee on a cold morning, the sound of rain on your window, or a kind word from a stranger. These small moments of goodness often go unnoticed, but when we take the time to appreciate them, they add up to a life that feels richer and more fulfilling.

IMPACT OF GRATITUDE

Increases Happiness: Research shows that people who regularly practice gratitude report higher levels of happiness and life satisfaction. Gratitude shifts our focus away from what we don't have, and helps us appreciate what we do.

Reduces Stress: Gratitude has been shown to reduce the production of stress hormones like cortisol. When we focus on what we're grateful for, we activate the brain's reward system, which leads to feelings of calm and relaxation.

Improves Relationships: Expressing gratitude, especially toward others, strengthens our relationships. People who regularly express thanks to their friends, family, and colleagues are more likely to experience stronger, more supportive connections.

Boosts Immune Function: Studies suggest that gratitude may even have a positive effect on our physical health. People who practice gratitude have been found to have stronger immune systems and experience fewer health problems.

Improves Sleep: Practicing gratitude before bed can improve the quality of your sleep. A study found that people who wrote down things they were grateful for before going to sleep experienced better, deeper rest.

HOW TO BE GRATEFUL?

Keep a Gratitude Journal

One of the most powerful ways to practice gratitude is by keeping a gratitude journal. Each day, take a few minutes to write down at least three things you're grateful for. These can be small or large, simple or profound—just things that bring you joy or remind you of the abundance in your life. Over time, this practice will help you develop a greater awareness of the good things around you.

Start Your Day with Gratitude

Before you even get out of bed, take a moment to reflect on what you're grateful for. This could be something as simple as feeling grateful for a good night's sleep or for the opportunity to start a new day. Setting this positive tone first thing in the morning can carry you through the rest of the day with a more optimistic mindset.

Express Your Gratitude to Others

One of the simplest and most effective ways to practice gratitude is by expressing it to others. Take the time to thank someone for their kindness, support, or just for being in your life. A simple "thank you" can go a long way in strengthening relationships and spreading positivity.

Practice Gratitude in Challenging Situations

It's easy to feel grateful when everything is going well, but practicing gratitude during difficult times can have an even greater impact. When faced with a challenge, try to find something to be grateful for, even if it's something small. For example, if you're dealing with stress at work, you might be grateful for the opportunity to learn and grow through the experience.

Use Gratitude Reminders

Incorporating reminders throughout your day can help you stay mindful of what you're grateful for. Place sticky notes with gratitude prompts on your desk, in your kitchen, or on your bathroom mirror. These little reminders can help shift your focus from what's going wrong to what's going right.

Reflect on Your Gratitude Before Bed

Before you fall asleep, take a moment to reflect on the things you're grateful for that day. This practice can help improve the quality of your sleep, as it shifts your mind away from stress and worries and toward a sense of peace and contentment.

Gratitude has the power to transform our thoughts, our emotions, and even our relationships. It's a practice that enriches our lives in ways we may not even fully realize at first. So take a moment each day to reflect on what you're grateful for. As you do, you'll begin to notice the beauty and abundance that surrounds you, and in turn, you'll begin to see that happiness was never about having more—it was about appreciating what you already have.

CHAPTER XI

MINDFULNESS

In a world that's constantly moving faster, with distractions at every turn, it's no wonder that many of us feel overwhelmed, anxious, and disconnected from the present moment. We live in a state of constant "doing" — rushing from task to task, planning for the future, or replaying the past in our minds. We are so busy that we forget to simply be.

This is where mindfulness comes in.

Mindfulness is the practice of being fully present and engaged in the here and now, without judgment. It's about cultivating awareness of our thoughts, emotions, and surroundings without getting lost in them. It's about noticing life as it unfolds, rather than rushing through it.

WHAT IS MINDFULNESS?

At its core, mindfulness is the art of paying attention. It means noticing your thoughts, feelings, and bodily sensations without judging them as good or bad. Mindfulness isn't about emptying your mind or trying to stop your thoughts. Rather, it's about observing them with curiosity and openness, allowing them to come and go without attaching to them.

Mindfulness can be practiced in many different ways — from meditation to simple everyday activities, like eating or walking. It's about shifting from autopilot mode to a state of awareness, where you're fully engaged with whatever you're doing in the moment. Whether you're sitting, standing, working, or interacting with others, mindfulness invites you to be fully present and aware.

HOW TO PRACTICE MINDFULNESS?

Mindful Breathing

One of the simplest ways to practice mindfulness is through mindful breathing. Find a quiet space where you can sit comfortably. Close your eyes and take a deep breath in, filling your lungs completely. As you exhale, notice how the air feels as it leaves your body. Focus on the sensation of the breath entering and leaving your body. If your mind starts to wander, gently bring your focus back to your breath. Try to do this for five minutes each day to help center your mind and calm your body.

Mindful Eating

Most of us eat on autopilot — rushing through meals or eating while distracted. Mindful eating involves slowing down and paying full attention to the experience of eating. Take the time to savor each bite, noticing the flavors, textures, and smells of your food. Engage all of your senses in the process of eating. This practice not only enhances your enjoyment of food, but it can also improve digestion and help you develop a healthier relationship with food.

Body Scan Meditation

A body scan is a mindfulness exercise where you mentally scan your body from head to toe, noticing any sensations, tension, or discomfort without judgment. Start by bringing your attention to your toes, then slowly move up through your feet, legs, torso, arms, and head. As you focus on each area, simply notice what you feel. This practice helps you become more attuned to your body and can be incredibly calming, especially if you're feeling stressed or anxious.

Mindful Walking

Walking can be a great way to practice mindfulness. As you walk, pay attention to the sensation of your feet touching the ground, the rhythm of your steps, and the movement of your body. Notice the sights, sounds, and smells around you, but without labeling them or getting caught up in thoughts. Simply observe. Mindful walking is a great practice for those who find it difficult to sit still for meditation or want to integrate mindfulness into their daily routine.

Mindfulness in Daily Activities

Mindfulness can also be practiced during everyday activities like washing dishes, folding laundry, or taking a shower. Instead of letting your mind wander to your to-do list or worries, focus on the task at hand. Notice the textures, sounds, and movements involved in each action. Bring your full awareness to the present moment, no matter how mundane the activity may seem.

Mindful Listening

Another powerful way to practice mindfulness is through mindful listening. When you're talking to someone, give them your full attention. Put away distractions, like your phone, and focus on really listening to what the other person is saying. Notice the tone of their voice, their body language, and the emotions behind their words. Mindful listening fosters deeper connections with others and improves communication.

OVERCOMING CHALLENGES

Here are some common challenges and tips for overcoming them:

Restlessness or Boredom: It's normal to feel restless or bored, especially when you first start practicing mindfulness. If you find your mind wandering or your body fidgeting, try to gently bring your focus back to your breath or the task at hand. With time and practice, your ability to stay present will improve.

Judging Your Thoughts: One of the biggest obstacles in mindfulness is judging our thoughts or emotions. You might think, "I shouldn't be feeling this way," or "I can't stop thinking about this." Remember, mindfulness is about observing without judgment. Simply notice your thoughts and let them pass without attaching any labels to them.

Finding Time: Many people struggle to find time for mindfulness practice in their busy lives. The truth is, mindfulness doesn't require hours of time — it can be practiced in small increments throughout your day. Start with just five minutes a day and gradually build up. You can practice mindfulness while commuting, washing dishes, or waiting in line.

Incorporating mindfulness into your daily life doesn't require perfection or special skills; it simply requires a willingness to be present. The more you practice mindfulness, the more you'll begin to notice the beauty, peace, and happiness that already exist around you.

So take a deep breath, slow down, and remember: happiness is not something you have to chase. It's right here, in the present moment, waiting for you to notice it.

CHAPTER XII

Self-Compassion – Embracing Yourself with Kindness

In the pursuit of happiness, there's one practice that can truly transform your relationship with yourself: self-compassion. It's easy to be kind and understanding to others, but when it comes to ourselves, we often fall into the trap of harsh self-criticism. We judge ourselves for our mistakes, our flaws, and our perceived shortcomings. We set impossible standards, expecting perfection, and when we inevitably fall short, we beat ourselves up.

But self-compassion offers a different way — a way that encourages us to treat ourselves with the same kindness, care, and understanding that we would offer to a close friend. It is the practice of acknowledging our pain, imperfection, and struggles with empathy rather than judgment. When we practice self-compassion, we stop being our own harshest critics and start becoming our own best supporters.

Many people struggle with self-compassion because they believe that it's selfish or indulgent. They worry that being kind to themselves will lead to laziness or complacency. However, research shows that self-compassion is not about letting yourself off the hook; it's about responding to yourself with care so that you can be more resilient and better equipped to face life's challenges.

Here are a few common barriers to self-compassion and ways to overcome them:

Fear of Being Selfish: Some people believe that self-compassion is the same as being self-centered or narcissistic. In truth, being compassionate toward yourself actually makes you more compassionate toward others. When you treat yourself with kindness, you are more likely to extend that same kindness to those around you.

Perfectionism: Perfectionists often struggle with self-compassion because they expect themselves to be flawless. The key here is to recognize that imperfection is part of the human experience. Practice embracing your flaws, knowing that they don't diminish your worth.

Difficulty with Forgiveness: It can be hard to forgive ourselves, especially if we've made significant mistakes. But self-compassion invites us to let go of guilt and shame. Forgiveness isn't about excusing our actions; it's about acknowledging that we are human and deserving of understanding.

CHAPTER XIII

Positive Habits – Building a Life of Joy and Fulfillment

Happiness doesn't just happen. It's something we create — through the choices we make, the actions we take, and the habits we build over time. Positive habits are the small, consistent actions that support our well-being, boost our mood, and lead us toward the life we desire. Just as negative habits can drain our energy and happiness, positive habits have the power to lift us up and sustain our joy.

WHY HABITS?

Habits are powerful because they shape our daily routines, and our routines create the foundation for our lives. The things we do every day — even the smallest actions — have a cumulative effect on our happiness. When we engage in positive habits consistently, we set ourselves up for long-term success and contentment. Here's why habits matter:

Habits Create Consistency

Positive habits provide structure and consistency. When we follow a routine that supports our well-being, we don't have to think about it — it becomes automatic. This consistency helps reduce stress and decision fatigue. Instead of trying to figure out what to do each day to improve your mood or mental state, positive habits make it easier to stay on track.

Habits Build Momentum

Once you start building positive habits, they begin to snowball. When you make progress in one area of your life — such as exercising regularly or practicing gratitude — it often leads to improvements in other areas. This momentum helps you feel more accomplished and motivated to keep going.

Habits Shape Our Identity

The habits we adopt reflect who we are and who we want to become. If you want to live a healthier, happier life, you need to start acting in ways that align with that vision. By building habits that promote well-being, you reinforce the identity of someone who values self-care, growth, and happiness.

Habits Improve Mental and Physical Health

Many positive habits — such as exercise, healthy eating, and practicing mindfulness — have direct benefits for both our physical and mental health. These habits improve our mood, reduce stress, enhance our energy levels, and promote a sense of well-being. By nurturing our bodies and minds through positive habits, we enhance our capacity for happiness.

Habits Foster Gratitude and Appreciation

Certain habits — like practicing gratitude or reflection — help us focus on the positive aspects of our lives. Instead of getting bogged down by negative thoughts, these habits help us cultivate an attitude of gratitude, which has been shown to improve overall happiness and life satisfaction.

HOW TO BUILD HABITS?

Building positive habits isn't always easy, but with the right approach, you can make lasting changes. The key is consistency, patience, and creating a supportive environment. Here are some steps to help you build habits that will stick:

Start Small

One of the biggest mistakes people make when trying to build new habits is starting too big. When we aim for dramatic change all at once, we often become overwhelmed or discouraged. Instead, start small. If your goal is to meditate every day, begin with just five minutes a day and gradually increase the time as you get more comfortable. Small, manageable steps make it easier to stay consistent and avoid burnout.

Make It Enjoyable

You're much more likely to stick to a new habit if you enjoy it. Find ways to make your new habits enjoyable and fun. If you want to exercise regularly, choose activities you love — whether that's dancing, hiking, or playing sports. If you want to practice mindfulness, experiment with different techniques until you find one that resonates with you. When habits feel good, you're more likely to stick with them.

Anchor New Habits to Existing Routines

One of the best ways to ensure a new habit sticks is to anchor it to something you already do regularly. This is known as "habit stacking." For example, if you already have a cup of coffee every morning, you could stack a five-minute gratitude practice immediately after your coffee. This approach helps you pair a new habit with something that is already ingrained in your routine, making it easier to remember and do.

Be Patient and Persistent

It takes time to build new habits — typically around 21 to 30 days for them to become automatic. Be patient with yourself during this process. There will be days when you miss a habit or when it feels difficult to stay motivated. The key is persistence. Don't beat yourself up if you miss a day; simply get back on track the next day and keep moving forward.

Track Your Progress

Tracking your progress helps keep you accountable and provides motivation to continue. You can keep a simple habit tracker where you mark off each day that you successfully complete your new habit. Seeing your progress visually can give you a sense of accomplishment and remind you of how far you've come.

Celebrate Your Wins

Every time you successfully complete a habit, no matter how small, celebrate your success. Recognizing your progress reinforces positive behavior and helps you feel motivated to keep going. Take a moment to acknowledge your efforts and give yourself credit for staying committed to building your new habits.

Cultivating habits can be difficult but you got to do what you got to do for yourself so these are habits that nurture your mind, body, and spirit, creating a foundation for lasting happiness.

Exercise Regularly

Physical activity has a profound effect on both our mental and physical health. Regular exercise releases endorphins, the body's natural "feel-good" chemicals, which boost mood and reduce stress. It also improves sleep, boosts energy, and supports overall well-being. Aim for at least 30 minutes of moderate exercise a few times a week.

Practice Gratitude

Gratitude is one of the most powerful tools for increasing happiness. By focusing on what you have, rather than what you lack, you shift your mindset toward positivity. Start a daily gratitude practice by writing down three things you're grateful for each day. Over time, this simple habit can have a profound impact on your outlook on life.

Practice Mindfulness

As discussed in the previous chapter, mindfulness is the practice of being present and fully engaged in the moment. Whether through meditation, mindful walking, or simply being aware of your breath, mindfulness helps reduce stress and anxiety, increases emotional regulation, and promotes a sense of calm and well-being.

Prioritize Sleep

Sleep is essential for both physical and mental health. A lack of sleep can lead to irritability, reduced focus, and a weakened immune system. Make sleep a priority by creating a relaxing bedtime routine, avoiding screens before bed, and setting a consistent sleep schedule. Aim for 7-9 hours of sleep each night.

Connect with Others

Strong, supportive relationships are one of the most significant contributors to happiness. Make time for meaningful connections with family, friends, and loved ones. Whether it's through a phone call, spending quality time together, or offering support during tough times, nurturing your relationships is essential for building happiness.

Practice Acts of Kindness

Doing something kind for others — whether it's a simple compliment, volunteering, or helping a neighbor — boosts your own happiness and creates a ripple effect of goodwill. Acts of kindness foster connection, promote positive emotions, and remind us of the good in the world.

Engage in Hobbies and Passions

Hobbies are an important part of life because they bring joy and fulfillment. Whether it's painting, reading, gardening, or playing an instrument, make time for activities that you genuinely enjoy. Engaging in passions outside of work or daily responsibilities helps recharge your energy and creates a sense of purpose.

Eat Nutritious Foods

The food we eat has a direct impact on our mood and

energy levels. Eating a balanced diet that includes plenty of fruits, vegetables, lean proteins, and healthy fats helps nourish our bodies and minds. Avoid excessive consumption of processed foods and sugar, as they can negatively impact your mood and energy.

Set Meaningful Goals

Having a sense of purpose and direction is crucial for happiness. Set goals that are aligned with your values and passions. Whether they're short-term or long-term, meaningful goals give you something to work toward and a sense of accomplishment when you achieve them.

Spend Time in Nature

Nature has a powerful impact on our well-being. Spending time outdoors, whether it's taking a walk in the park or hiking in the mountains, helps reduce stress, boosts mood, and enhances creativity. Try to incorporate time in nature into your routine to reap its mental and physical benefits.

CHAPTER XIV

The Power of Perspective – Shifting Your View to Cultivate Happiness

How we perceive the world and our experiences has an enormous impact on our emotional well-being. Two people can go through the exact same event or challenge, yet their reactions and emotions can be completely different, all because of the way they choose to interpret that situation. Perspective isn't just about seeing things clearly — it's about choosing to see things in a way that supports your happiness and well-being.

To understand how powerful a shift in perspective can be, consider these examples:

<u>From Failure to Growth</u>: Imagine someone who has just faced a major setback at work, such as being passed over for a promotion. Instead of dwelling on the disappointment and feeling like a failure, they shift their perspective to view the situation as an opportunity for personal growth. They may seek feedback, work on developing new skills, and approach the next opportunity with a sense of readiness and confidence. This shift in perspective allows them to turn a negative situation into a springboard for future success.

<u>From Stress to Calm:</u> Another example is someone who faces a stressful situation, like a tight deadline at work. Instead of letting the pressure overwhelm them, they shift their perspective by viewing the situation as a challenge rather than a threat. They break the task down into smaller, manageable steps, focus on one thing at a time, and approach the challenge with a calm, problem-solving mindset. This shift in perspective helps reduce their stress and allows them to perform more effectively.

<u>From Loneliness to Connection:</u> A person who feels lonely might shift their perspective by focusing on the potential for connection rather than dwelling on their isolation. They could choose to reach out to a friend, volunteer, or join a new group activity. By changing how they view their social situation, they open themselves up to new opportunities for connection and support.

The power of perspective lies in its ability to shape our experience of life. By shifting how we view ourselves, others, and the world, we can create more joy, resilience, and fulfillment. A positive perspective doesn't mean ignoring challenges or pretending everything is perfect — it means choosing

The Path Forward

As we come to the close of this journey together, I want to leave you with one simple truth: Happiness is not a destination. It's a practice. It's a collection of small, intentional choices you make every day — choices that align with your values, your purpose, and your truest self.

Throughout The Happiness Project, we've explored the many facets of happiness — from the power of mindset to the importance of cultivating healthy habits, from the value of self-compassion to the need for deep, meaningful connections. Each chapter has revealed that happiness isn't something that happens to us; it's something we create through our actions, our thoughts, and the way we choose to respond to life's challenges.

But even more than that, we've learned that happiness is not about perfection. It's about embracing the present moment, finding joy in the journey, and learning how to navigate both the light and the shadow of life with grace. It's about showing up for yourself — with all of your flaws, your imperfections, and your beautiful humanity — and choosing to be kind, patient, and loving along the way.

The practices and strategies we've discussed are not one-size-fits-all solutions. They are tools for you to experiment with and make your own. You are the author of your own happiness. You hold the pen, and it's up to you to write the story. While external circumstances will always be a part of life, the way you choose to interpret and respond to those circumstances is where your power lies.

As you move forward, I encourage you to remember that happiness is a lifelong journey. There will be days when you feel on top of the world, and there will be days when you feel down or uncertain. That's okay. It's all part of the human experience. The key is to approach each day with curiosity, compassion, and an openness to learn and grow. By doing so, you will cultivate a deep and lasting sense of fulfillment that comes not from what you achieve, but from how you live.

So, take a deep breath, acknowledge the progress you've made, and remember: You are already on your way. No matter where you are in life, no matter what challenges you face, you have the power to choose happiness in every moment. It's not about waiting for the perfect circumstances. It's about finding joy in the present, creating moments of peace in the chaos, and trusting that happiness is something you can nurture — right here, right now.

The happiness you seek is already within you. It's waiting for you to step into it, embrace it, and make it your own.

Thank you for taking this journey with me. May you continue to grow, evolve, and live a life full of the happiness you truly deserve.